In loving memory of David Broehl,

who gave so much to so many —M.C.

To Arthur and Leonardo, who recently

gave the world their first smiles —F.S.

Text copyright © 2022 by Marcy Campbell
Jacket art and interior illustrations copyright © 2022 by Francesca Sanna

All rights reserved. Published in the United States by Alfred A. Knopf,
an imprint of Random House Children's Books,
a division of Penguin Random House LLC, New York.

Knopf, Borzoi Books, and the colophon are registered trademarks of
Penguin Random House LLC.

Visit us on the Web! rhcbooks.com

Educators and librarians, for a variety of teaching tools,
visit us at RHTeachersLibrarians.com

Library of Congress Cataloging-in-Publication Data
Names: Campbell, Marcy, author. | Sanna, Francesca, illustrator.
Title: The more you give / Marcy Campbell, Francesca Sanna.
Description: First edition. | New York: Alfred A. Knopf, 2022. | Audience: Ages 4–8 |
Audience: Grades K–1 | Summary: "A modern-day response to The Giving Tree,
this lyrical picture book shows how family love is passed down from generation to generation."
—Provided by publisher.
Identifiers: LCCN 2021028119 | ISBN 978-0-593-37273-9 (hardcover) |
ISBN 978-0-593-37274-6 (library binding) | ISBN 978-0-593-37275-3 (ebook)
Subjects: CYAC: Picture books. | Families—Fiction. | Love—Fiction. | Trees—Fiction. | LCGFT: Picture books.
Classification: LCC PZ7.1.C336 Mo 2022 | DDC [Fic]—dc23

The text of this book is set in 17-point ITC Usherwood.
The illustrations were created using digital painting tools.
Book design by Nicole Gastonguay

MANUFACTURED IN CHINA
August 2022
10 9 8 7 6 5 4 3 2 1
First Edition

The More You Give

Marcy Campbell   Francesca Sanna

ALFRED A. KNOPF
New York

Once there was a wide-open field
and a boy who loved his grandmother,
who loved him back.

And they were happy.

The grandmother gave
the boy many gifts,
like big hugs,

and bigger laughter, and the very biggest Sunday-morning pancakes.

But she had more to give.
Small gifts, like acorns,
tiny and shiny, with wild and woolly caps.

Most of the gifts she gave to the boy
were ones that he could not hold in his hands.

Like all of her wisdom
about how things grow.

The boy watched and wondered
until one day . . .

. . . oh!

"When will it be bigger than me?" he asked as he dreamed of swings and secret spaces.

In reply, his grandmother gave him another gift . . . patience.

The boy had a birthday, and the tree reached his knees.

The boy had a birthday, and the tree reached his shoulders.

The boy's grandmother had
a birthday, and he gave her
many gifts,
like a poem, a picture,
a crown, and, most of all,
his love.

And she
loved him back.
And they
were happy.

Until one day . . .

. . . oh.

Slowly, slowly,

happiness spread its roots again.
The boy's grandmother had taught him
to ask for help when he needed it.
And so, remembering, he did.

He watered and weeded while

he watched and wondered.

He grew tall with wondering,
still dreaming of swings
and secret spaces.

But not for himself.

Once there was a not-so-wide-open field
and a girl who loved her father,
who loved her back.

And they were happy.

The father gave the girl many gifts, like piggyback rides,

and plump strawberries,

and bedtime stories about his grandmother.

He also gave the girl acorns—
tiny, shiny things with
wild and woolly caps.

But he had more to give,
like all of his wisdom
about how things grow.

"When will it be bigger than me?" the girl asked. And he explained how love, even when given to the smallest of things, can spread, up and out, and grow bigger than she could ever imagine.

Together, they watered
and weeded, and in time,
they found shade,
a home, and strong,
thick branches that were
perfect for . . .

. . . oh!

They watched and waited and wondered.
The girl grew,
and the trees grew,
and their love grew and spread, up and out,
while the girl dreamed of secret spaces.

But not for herself.

Once there was a field, dotted with trees,
and a boy who loved his mother,
who loved him back.

And they were happy.

The boy's mother gave him
pancakes made from her
great-grandmother's recipe,
topped with strawberries
from her father's patch,

and hugs
and laughter

and piggyback rides and

bedtime stories
about their family

and its love
of green,
growing things.

The boy's mother gave him acorns,
and together they planted,

and watered and weeded,

and watched and wondered.

From their secret space,
which wasn't very secret,
the boy and his mother
shared their wisdom,

with anyone and everyone,
about how things grow,
like trees,
and people,
and kindness.

The boy always had
more love to give,
and he got love in return.
Was it bigger than him?
It was.

It was much bigger than
he had ever imagined.

And that is why
he was happy.

Once there was a forest . . .